By an Ex-Condederate Officer

The Tyrant of New Orleans

A drama

By an Ex-Condederate Officer

The Tyrant of New Orleans
A drama

ISBN/EAN: 9783337343958

Printed in Europe, USA, Canada, Australia, Japan

Cover: Foto ©Andreas Hilbeck / pixelio.de

More available books at **www.hansebooks.com**

THE

ʔYRANT OF ЙEW ʘRLEANS.

A DRAMA.

By an Ex-Confederate Officer.

ATLANTA, GA.

Published by " The Herald" Publishing Company.

1873.

NOTE.

The real characters represented in this piece are personally unknown to the Author, and none of them have been consulted by him as to the use of their names.

For the liberty he has taken, he craves pardon of such of them as " play the better part."

DRAMATIS PERSONÆ.

Major General B. F. Butler, commanding Gulf Dep't.
A. J. Butler, brother of Gen. Butler.
Col. Geo. C. Strong, A. A. Gen. and Chief of Staff.
Capt. Davis, A. A. A. Gen.; Capt. Brennan. and other
  Staff officers.
Colonel James H. French, Provost Marshal and Chief of
  Police.
Maj. H. C. Whitley, Chief of Detective Police.
John T. Munro, Mayor of New Orleans.
W. B. Mumford, citizen of New Orleans.
Mrs. Mumford, wife of W. B. Mumford.
Miss Mumford, daughter of W. B. Mumford.
Mrs. Philips, wife of Philip Philips, of New Orleans.
Mrs. Campbell, a Lady of New Orleans.
Mr. and Mrs. Martell, of New Orleans.
Auguste Beaumont, a wealthy Creole of New Orleans.
Eugene Beaumont, son of Auguste Beaumont.
Clarence Rennier, a Confederate Soldier.
Belle Beaumont, daughter of Auguste Beaumont.

Guards. sentinels, orderlies, citizens, and
other attendants.

THIS HUMBLE EFFORT

Of an inexperienced hand to portray,

in the form of the Drama,

The character of one who has achieved an

UNENVIABLE IMMORTALITY,

IS RESPECTFULLY DEDICATED

by the Author,

To those who FELT MOST KEENLY,

AND SUFFERED MOST BY, HIS ACTS OF TYRANNY,

The Ladies of New Orleans.

TYRANT OF NEW ORLEANS.

ACT I.

SCENE I.

New Orleans. A street.

(Enter citizens.)

1st cit. The latest news, friend?

2d cit. The Yankee fleet has passed the forts—will soon be opposite the city, just as I expected.

1st cit. Have the forts surrendered?

2d cit. All I know is that the Yankee fleet will soon have us under its guns, just as I expected.

1st cit. Expected! Why I thought our means of defense ample. We have certainly had that assurance. The forts have been represented impregnable; and then the gunboats, we all know, were most formidable.

2d cit. The enemy's fleet, I tell you, is nearing the city. The gunboats you mention were not completed.

1st cit. Where is Gen. Lovell with his command?

2d cit. Gen. Lovell! with his fifteen hundred or two thousand men and no works on the river front worth a groat, to contend with Farragut's fleet!—nonsense!

1st cit. Then what are we to do?

2d cit. Do! Why what can we do, but surrender? Just as I expected we would have to do.

1st cit. Burn the city first.

2d cit. Pray, what good would that do?

1st cit. It would not then fall into the hands of the enemy.

2d cit. That all? Nonsense! Turn the women and children out of doors, and destroy millions of property, and for what? To gratify a mere impulse?

1st cit. (Looking in direction), I see a great light towards the river. The city, I verily believe, is now on fire.

2d cit. Merciful heavens; what madness! just as I expected.

(Enter other citizens.)

What fire is that?

3d cit. Cotton burning on the wharves.

2d cit. Where is General Lovell?

3d cit. Just come up from the Forts, and is now evacuating the city, with his command—every thing, my friend, is gone up.

2d cit. Gone *down*, I should say.

3d cit. Mutiny in Fort Jackson lost us all.

2d cit. Mutiny in Fort Jackson?

3d cit. Aye!

2d cit. Just as I expected! When the State seceded, I went with her, but I knew it was bad policy. I never believed that our people would stand up to this thing. It has turned out just as I expected.

3d cit. He is a poor prophet whose predictions are fulfilled ere they are made known. But expected or not, New Orleans will be occupied by the enemy. Old Hickory is not here to turn cotton bags into breast-works, and fight to the last, firing the hearts of his soldiers with the enemy's battle-cry, " Beauty and Booty!" No! our army now burns the cotton, and runs away.

2d cit. My friend, no good could come of fighting. The guns of the fleet would demolish the city in a few hours. General Lovell is right.

3d cit. That may be; but I would at least give them a few rounds, if for nothing more than to let them know that there were a few brave men left here. By-the-way, it is said that Gen. Butler is in command of the land forces, and will be the military Commander of the Department.

2d cit. Then we may fare better than was supposed. General Butler was a Democrat before the War. He was a delegate to the National Democratic Convention which assembled in Charleston, and voted sixty times for Jeff Davis for the Presidency.

3d cit. Tush! so much the worse for us. The zeal of new converts is proverbial. Gen. Butler will out-herod Herod in his cruel treatment of our people. It is the nature of men to hate those whom they have betrayed. He will prove no exception to the rule

(Enter another citizen.)

The latest news?

4th cit. Mayor Munro refused the demand for the surrender of the city; but a naval officer with a company of marines landed, and hoisted the United States flag upon the Mint, and then retired to the fleet. I have since heard that some of our men are preparing to haul the flag down.

1st cit. I pray that they may. If that flag should not be lowered, may it float only over the ashes of the city.

3d cit. My sentiments.

4th cit. And mine.

('Two guns fired from the fleet.)

1st cit. Firing upon the city! Let us hurry to the scene. [*Exeunt* citizens.

SCENE II.

St. Charles Hotel. Gen. Butler's Headquarters. New Orleans.

(Enter Gen. Butler and Col. Strong, A. A. General and Chief of Staff.)

Gen. B. Made no effort at escape! He must be a most daring rebel.

Col. S. Major Whitley had no difficulty in finding his place of residence; he bore his arrest quietly—indeed most defiantly.

Gen. B. Before he is committed have the guard bring him here; I would speak with him.

Col. S. He shall be brought immediately into your presence. [*Exit* Col. Strong.

Gen. B. Whitley has met the occasion promptly ;
The villain who tore down his country's flag,
And with trait'rous hands trail'd it in the dust !
Mumford shall not escape the punishment
Due this most audacious act of treason,

(Enter guard with Mumford in irons.)

Gen. B. (Addressing Mumford.)
In tearing down from yonder staff the flag,
Which is the ensign of thy country's power,
Thou hast committed an act of treason;
Thou art not now on trial before me ;
That is reserv'd for other tribunal ;
I would not wound thy feelings, nor deny
Thy right to a fair trial for this crime ;
But I would, before the door of thy cell
Is closed against thee, have thee tell me,
What hellish motive led thee to this act ?
Why insult thy country's flag and my pow'r ?
Mumford. To discuss with the Commanding General
My guilt or innocence when he decides
That question before I have a hearing,
Would seem a bootless waste of breath and time ;
He says that I am guilty of treason ;
After judgment, sentence is all that's left.
Gen. B. My opinion amounts not to judgment ;
That will be passed by the court of trial ;
What I mean to say, is *prima facie*
Thou art guilty, and must acquit thyself.
Mumford. Manacled thus, silence becomes me most,
But loose these shackles, and thou mayst hear me,
If such be thy wish, as to the motive
That prompted the act which thou call'st treason.
Gen. B. Take his irons off.   (Done by guard.)
Mumford. At thy request, I now defend myself
Against the odious charge thou hast prefer'd ;
I am not a traitor to my country ;
'Twas not *my* country's flag this hand haul'd down;
My country is my own Louisiana ;
To her only is my allegiance due ;
My flag is the one she and her sisters
Flung to the breeze in freedom's holy cause—
And may its stars and bars and azure cross,
Continue to float proudly on the winds—
A terror to tyrants and the patriot's pride.
Gen. B. Hold, sir ; in my very presence you affirm
your treason.
Mumford. You ask me to speak in my defence and
then silence me ?

Gen. B. Proceed sir; if your folly convicts you, the
act that condemns you is yours, not mine. You invite
judgment against yourself.

Mumford. 'Tis not the judgment of man the brave fear;
It is the voice of avenging conscience—
Its thunder peals which 'rive the cow'ring soul,
They fear, and the peace its approval brings
In life's trials and sorrows, they ne'er forget;
I am shielded by a guiltless conscience
For the act thou art pleas'd to call treason.
When thy country's ensign this hand haul'd down,
The city had not yet been surrender'd;
Then, 'twas not treason—but an act of war,
War waged between belligerent powers,
The one striking for right and liberty,
The other, for spoils, and power, and conquest;
In such case, duty could not hesitate;
To my State my all, life itself belong'd;
If for this thou would'st claim the sacrifice;
Prepare the altar; here is thy victim;
Honor, truth, fidelity to country—
These are the brightest jewels in the crown,
Which men win on earth, to wear in heaven.

Gen. B. Take the prisoner to his cell. Let there be
no communication with him except through these
Headquarters. The Adjutant General will issue the
order. [*Exit* guard with Mumford.

Gen. B. (strikes his bell; enters orderly.) Bid Col.
Strong come to me immediately. [*Exit* orderly.

(Enter Col. Strong.)

Gen. B. Have you the Military Commission, which
was ordered, fully organized?

Col. S. I have.

Gen. B. Then, have Mumford put upon trial immediately. I must make a speedy example of him; he is still
most defiant in his treason. [*Exit* Col. Strong.

Gen. B. (Solus.)
Now that the Stars and Stripes do proudly float
O'er this rebel city, and trait'rous hands,
Unnerv'd, no longer raise the vile standard
Of revolt, a time for prudent thought arrives,
When we must our policy determine;
What best we may do to crush out treason,
And our own wants and interests advance;

How selfish ends may be best promoted,
While all may be laid to love of country.
Politics is my trade; I play soldier,
Not martial, but civic honors, to win,
And what the o'er righteous call filthy lucre;
With gold, ambition bribes Fortune herself;
Wisdom's plans without it, are abortions ;
Poverty has been call'd ambition's spur ;
Rather should it be call'd its nightmare ;
Astride of genius and valor sitting,
It smothers their noblest thoughts and aims.
I once stood by the South, her champion,
Her rights and honor boldly defending
Against the cry of mad fanaticism,
Hounded to its work by fell ambition ;
True, self-interest, then, as now, was my aim ;
But the time is past when to speak the truth,
And defend the right, lead on to fortune.
Patriotism ! why it's become a bye-word !
Who, for his conduct, claims this the motive,
Is accounted ill-suited to the times—
A fool who would make himself a martyr
To mawkish sentiment or foolish pride;
Now, to this school I claim not to belong;
I'm for myself first—for my country next ;
My own safety, too, must be first thought of;
To cool down the South's hot blood by honied words,
Or bait it with treason, were indeed vain ;
What surety have I 'gainst treach'rous steel,
Or poison, or any machination,
That may be invented to take me off,
A victim of malice or mad revenge ?
The coat of mail this body doth encase,
Is not sure proof against the dagger's point;
This is an age of cunning inventions,
Which may serve to trick the devil himself.
It then behooves me to be most watchful,
By sword and bayonet hedge myself in,
And cut off ev'ry approach of treason,
Thus, gaining sense of real security ;
This done, with the mail'd hand of power,
The stiff necks of this people I will bend
In submission to my purpose and will,
And shew them what I am—a Conqueror.

ACT II.

SCENE I.

St. Charles Hotel, New Orleans.   Gen. Butler seated at
his desk, writing.

(Enter A. J. Butler.)

Gen. B. A timely call, I am glad you have come ;
We must proceed to execute our plans
On this new theatre with due despatch.
You know I'm not much in favor at Court ;
I am not esteem'd there, and my service
Is prized only for its worth to others,
In this extremity of cruel war ;
The only security of place I have
Is success, and that is most uncertain ;
War is, at best, a doubtful game to play ;
Too often mere chance decides the battle ;
And fell ambition is ever at work
To undo them who fortune's favors win.
'Tis true here I have no battles to fight,
But only to rule a conquer'd city,
To my taste a duty more congenial,
But as difficult as field strategy,
Having nothing of its martial glory ;
The juncture I fully estimate ;
I must use it to the best advantage,
And while opportunity is offer'd,
Seize its golden moments ere they are gone.
The poet has nothing more wisely said,
Than " we must take the current when it serves,
Or lose our ventures."

A. J. B. I have felt the importance of hastening the
execution of our plans, and have already made some
progress.   I have made arrangements which, with your
authority, I have no doubt will secure a large quantity
of cotton from our rebel brethren.   For arms and other
war material, the exchange may be made.   You know
that you suggested this plan to me.

Gen. B. Yes, but it is a delicate business, and must

be managed with great tact. You must be certain that you know with whom you are dealing.

A. J. B. I understand that, and will use due caution to guard against deception.

Gen. B. An order has been issued by Governor Shelby, authorizing the organization of volunteers in this department, and Major Whitley has been appointed to that duty. To forward the business you suggest, let him make requisitions on the Ordnance officers for arms and ammunition—I will approve it. Instructions will be given as to their destination. In all future transactions of this kind, let this be the plan. Get all the cotton you can; consign it to our factors in New York and Boston ; make your principal consignments to Boston. By means of requisitions upon the different departments, supplies of all kinds may be exchanged for cotton. The necessity for the distribution of commissary stores amongst the poor of this city and the Department, will also open the door for transactions of this kind. Permits, covering transportations of military stores, will be given. In this business, be extremely cautious, and we may realize great gains. I will give Major Whitley the necessary instructions. He will act in concert with us.

[*Exit* A. J. B.

(Enter Col. French, Provost Marshal.)

Gen. B. I am glad you have called. Allow me to congratulate you upon your success in scenting out the traitors who lurk in the hiding places of this city, and in bringing them to justice. You must have an efficient detective police.

Col. F. Yes, I am fortunate in having a man at its head who understands his duty, and has the nerve to do it.

Gen. B. Whittey is no doubt master of his calling.

Col. F. By the way, he was in waiting for an interview with you when I came in. My object, General, in calling at this time, is to report an important arrest, a rebel soldier, charged with being a spy within our lines. Another arrest would have been made, but the person had not entirely recovered from wounds received in battle, and it was thought best not to move him till a surgeon reported on his case. He was however left under guard.

Gen. B. Who are these persons ?

Col. F. The person arrested calls himself Clarence
Rennier.   He was found at the house of one Auguste
Beaumont, and his son is the person left under guard.

Gen. B. How was this arrest procured ?

Col. F. The information came from the detective police office.

Gen. B. Then send Major Whitley to me ; he is no
doubt acquainted with the facts of the case.

[*Exit* Col. French.

(Enter Maj. Whitley.)

Maj. W. Your most obedient servant.   General, I
come at your bidding, but was at the time seeking au-
dience with you.

Gen. B. Welcome; you have heretofore proved yourself an expert in unraveling the skein of crime, and in
bringing offenders to justice, but you have never before
set your hand to work like that in which you are now
engaged.   It is not with ordinary criminals, mere vio-
lators of the municipal law, those who trample upon the
rights of their fellow-men that you are dealing, but with
the public enemy—traitors, who with unholy hands seek
to destroy the best government on earth, and involve
our country in anarchy, and enthrone discord where
peace and order should reign supreme ; men who would
haul down our flag, and trail it in the dust.   I am glad
to know that you are taking these political malefactors
by the throat.   I congratulate you upon your success in
the good work.   In this service you are to obey my orders and report to me.   The Provost Marshal must not
be deprived of all semblance of authority—that would
be humiliating, and breed dissension.   An eye must be
had to that—forms must be adhered to.   But hear me ;
I am to be your chief, and direct your business.   The
expedient of flattering others with a show of authority,
may sometimes serve a purpose—that is for me to determine.   Your secrets are to be mine, and none others.
My plans are to be worked according to my orders,
whether given publicly or secretly.

Maj. W. I will render cheerful and prompt obedience
to your instructions and orders, at all times and under
all circumstances.   It is only necessary for them to be
made known to me.

Gen. B. What means the arrest of these persons
charged with being spies ?

Maj. W. I was just on my way to report to you the facts of the case. I was present when the arrest was made. I got the information about these young men from a resident loyalist, who sought a secret interview with me. He is by the way, a confounded shrewd fellow. In doing loyal service, he would, at the same time, drive a bargain for himself, tho' he would have it understood that he is actuated by feelings of patriotism.

Gen. B. The fellow talks about patriotism, eh ? He don't know that's played out ? Who the devil is he ?

Maj. W. Well, (smiling) he is a Down-Easter from Massachusetts.

Gen. B. His nativity commends his honesty and patriotism, does'nt it ? I don't care to know his name. If I scent the game, I leave the matter entirely to you and my brother. You are to manage these outside affairs. What do you suppose the fellow wants ?

Maj. W. No doubt a share of the ransom that may be offered.

Gen. B. That will be considered ; it will depend much upon the amount of the offer. See my brother. You and he will manage this affair.

Maj. W. I have seen him on the subject, but will see him again. As I have already stated, I was present when the arrest was made ; indeed, I had it made. It was claimed that the condition of one of the young men was such that it would be dangerous to move him, he having received wounds in battle from which he had not recovered. The father, and perhaps the daughter, who, by the way, in her tears, appeared as beautiful as the rose wet with the morning dew, will, no doubt, call to intercede for the son and his friend. I understand so. He is a rich old Creole, a retired merchant, I believe. He numbers his houses by the hundred. His stocks and public securities are fabulous in amount ; and, then, his gold and silver plate is described to be, in style and value, equal to any owned in this luxurious Southern city. Besides, his cellars are filled with the choicest wines and brandies—of the oldest vintages, and his walls are adorned with paintings of the old masters. I have all needful information. We have a rich prize, indeed— no richer in all the city.

Gen. B. You say he has costly plate, fine paintings, gold and silver ?

Maj. W. My dear General, it is a princely establishment. His treasure is no doubt secreted, but it can be found. He can be made disgorge it.

Gen. B. I have no transportation for houses, and bank stocks and other securities may prove worthless—even the bonds of our own Government. Gold and silver—they are substantial things, even though in spoons—an insignificant article of domestic economy. But the old gentleman may spirit his money and valuables away, that's the danger. You and my brother must look to this. [*Exit* Whitley.

Gen. B. (Solus.) This fellow will be invaluable to me. He is the shrewdest, most unscrupulous rascal I have ever met with. But such instruments I need here. Now, the *denouement* of this affair I can't exactly foresee, but there is money in it; and to that end I will give it countenance. I don't intend that the Quartermasters and Commissaries shall do all the stealing in my Department—or rather, make all the money. But I must operate through others—I may shuffle and pack the cards—others must play the game.

(Enter Col. Strong.)

Col. S. I have some papers, General, which require your signature. (Hands papers to Gen. B., who signs them.)

Gen. B. I was about sending for you. I am obliged to notice the insults which the women of this city are hourly offering the officers and men of my command. These "bejewelled, becrinolined, and laced creatures calling themselves ladies," allow no opportunity to pass without treating us with contempt. Why, they turn up their noses at me as I pass the streets. If they treat me in this way, what may not be expected of their treatment of my inferiors? I will teach these "she-adders" a lesson. I have prepared a general order on the subject, which you will have published in all the city papers. I will read it: (reads.)

"GENERAL ORDER NO. 28.

As the officers and soldiers of the United States have been subject to repeated insults from the women (calling themselves ladies) of New Orleans, in return for the most scrupulous non-interference and courtesy on our part, it is ordered that hereafter, when any female shall

by word, gesture or movement, insult or show contempt
for any officer or soldier of the United States, she shall
be regarded as a Woman of the Town, plying her voca-
tion." (Hands the order to Col. Strong, who reads it
standing, then seats himself and reperuses it in silence.)

Col. S. General, this order will produce quite a commotion. It is a very important one. Have you given it
your usual thought and reflection ?

Gen. B. I have, sir ; and have it published as I tell
you, and just as it is written.

SCENE II.

Headquarters, St. Charles Hotel.

Gen. B. (Solus.) My position is a most difficult one;
I'm damn'd by the rebels around me,
Cursed as a tyrant—for all that is bad ;
And then at Washington, I have few friends ;
Lincoln has his partizans to advance,
I am not of them, and there lies the rub.
Before the war I was a Democrat ;
The abolition movement I refus'd to join ;
The mad enthusiasts who began it
Were courted for party ends—nothing more ;
The good of the poor slave was least thought of ;
It was pow'r, office, ambition's schemes
Which with fanaticism sought alliance,
And, in the end, the Union disrupted ;
In this dread work I took no part ;
But when the war came, the safer ground I chose ;
I saw it was the time to jump the game,
And was right glad it came so opportune.
I knew that the North would never consent
That these States be allow'd to go in peace ;
That blood and tears—all the horrors of war—
From this resolve would not move its people ;
And with them my fortunes I sought to cast ;
But my success is view'd with jealous eyes,
Because, in the past, I championed the South.
This is my offence, and now all my acts
Will meet with scrutiny, and be measur'd
By the standard of party interest.
My only hope is my people's support ;
My tactics now must be so directed

As to stir their hearts to the highest pitch
Of hate and revenge towards these people;
To this end, I'll now champion the negro,
And by every art treason be made appear
As black and damning as Hell itself.
Orderly, (enters orderly) Brandy and water, sir.
    (Serves the same.)   [*Exit* Orderly.

(Enter Auguste Beaumont and Belle Beaumont, sentinel
following.)

   A Beaumont. (Giving his own name and his daughter's, addressing Gen. B.)
A father's love has brought an old man here
To plead for a son, held now in durance;
If he be guilty of any offence,
I know it not, except it be the crime
Of answer'ng the call of his native State,
And taking up arms to defend her soil;
He has just return'd from the battle field,
Sorely wounded, and, it may be, to die;
His companion in arms, who was his guest
At my house, has been already taken;
And he, out of pity, left under guard.
   Gen. B. (Interrupting abruptly) Sir, the case has already been reported to me.
   Aug. B. Pray tell me what is the charge against my son?
   Gen. B. Respect for gray hairs only prompts an answer—I should have added, and woman's presence, (turning to Miss B.) Your son and his companion are charged not only with treason, but with being spies. They are enemies within my lines. You know the punishment to which spies are exposed by the rules of war.
   Aug. B. Great God, my son a spy! Is it possible that he is accused of this? Why, General, he was here when the city was occupied. He and Capt. Rennier were wounded at Shiloh, where the great Johnston fell; were brought here then, and have remained here since; they were unable to leave. They are no spies; the accusation is false.
   Gen. B. What about the treason? Your own lips smack of that, and I suppose that you are proud of the crime of your son against his country?
   Aug. B. If obedience to the call of his State to defend her rights be treason, my son's guilt is manifest.

But, do you propose to put all, who have borne arms
against the United States Government and fall into your
hands, upon trial for that offence?

Gen. B. That may be—I do not answer the question.
You have seen my order requiring the oath of allegiance
to the United States Government to be taken by all.
Has your son obeyed this order? That might save him
from punishment as a traitor to his country, but not as a
spy. He is now held under both these charges, and he
shall be tried for them, and if convicted, shall suffer the
penalty of his crime. I have no leniency to offer the
stiff-necked people of this city. Clemency, humanity,
generosity—the exercise of these virtues towards them,
would only make them more incorrigible—still greater
rebels. No, I shall have to use the strong arm of military power, without mercy, to bring them back to loyal
ways—to make them respect my authority and the Government I represent. This interview is to no purpose, if
you hope that any thing you may say, will relax my
hand in this case. If found guilty, these young men
shall die the death they deserve. Young woman, you
may dry your tears—with me they will avail nothing.
You women of New Orleans will expose yourselves to a
fate worse than the death of brothers or lovers, if you
continue the course you are now pursuing towards the
officers and soldiers of my command.

[*Exeunt* Aug. Beaumont and daughter.

(Enter Col. Strong.)

Col. S. I have to report that all the city papers refuse
to publish General Order No. 28, and that I have been
compelled to give it publicity by placarding it in the
streets.

Gen. B. Refused to publish my orders! Then they
shall publish nothing! Order their offices closed. I
will have their type thrown into the river, and the pro-
prietors put in Fort Jackson. That will bring them to
their senses. Defy my authority in this manner! This
is an overt act of treason. They shall publish Order No.
28, or any other that I may require.

ACT III.

SCENE 1.

(Enter Col. Strong with Mayor Munro and citizens, an-
nouncing them to Gen. Butler, who is seated at his
desk writing.)   [*Exit* Col. Strong.

Gen. B. (Leaving visitors standing.)   To what am I
indebted for the honor of this call ?

Mayor M. Your General Order No. 28, which has
been placarded in the city, has produced a profound
sensation ; and at the instance of many of our best citizens, ladies and gentlemen, we have sought this interview for the purpose of asking a revocation, or at least a
qualification of that order. That is the object of our
call.

Gen. B. Ask me to revoke an order ! What assurance ! and coming, too, from such a source, at least, as
far as you take part in it, Mr. Mayor ! You ! who when
this city, whose fortunes were in your hands, was at the
mercy of our guns, refused to surrender it, and take
down your rebel flag ; nay, further, allowed our flag,
your country's flag, after it had been hoisted on your
Mint, by order of Flag Officer Farragut, to be hauled
down, and before your own eyes trailed in the dust and
torn into shreds by rebel hands ; You, who exposed the
lives and property of your citizens, women and children,
to destruction ; You, who, to the last, affirmed in terms
of defiance, your own, and the allegiance of your people
to the so-called Confederate States ; You, after this conduct, and when your city has been spared by a merciful
Conqueror, now have the assurance to come here, and
ask the revocation or qualification of one of my orders,
which was provoked by your own conduct, and made
necessary to protect my men and officers from wrong
and insult ; if this be not the climax of bare-faced ef-
frontery, I know not the meaning of the terms.

Mayor M. We have not come here, General, to vin-
dicate our own conduct, or the conduct of our fellow-
citizens, either before or since the occupation of the city.
Our object, as I have already stated, is to confer with

you as to the qualification of this order.   It has alarmed
our citizens, especially females. They fear that by it
they are exposed to insult and outrage.   It is to quiet
their fears chiefly, that we seek the modification of the
order.

Gen. B. I don't want to quiet their fears: My object
was to excite their fears. This is the only way to reach
their rebel hearts, and humble their pride.   They have
treated my officers and men with contempt, aye, spit
upon them, and by their own conduct provoked insult.
They shall be subject to the deepest humiliation.   If
politeness and good breeding are not sufficient to control
their conduct, I will make fear the restraint.   You and
your co-adjutors are, in a great measure, responsible for
this state of feeling amongst the women.   Men should
control their wives and daughters. If they cannot, they
are not much of men.   But you don't want to control
them. You hide yourselves behind their petticoats. No;
that order was well considered, and deliberately issued ;
and it shall stand as it is ; I shall not abate one word of
it, and your city newspapers shall publish it, or every
one of them shall be stopped. If you have no other
business, this interview may be well allowed to close.

[*Exeunt* Mayor Munroe and citizens.

SCENE II.

Auguste Beaumont's house, New Orleans.   Present—A.
Beaumont, his daughter Belle, and son Eugene, who
is reclining on couch with crutches in his hand.

Aug. B. Well, poor Mumford's trial is over, and he
is of course convicted. What else could have been
looked for ?

Belle B. We have heard so, father, and execution
will surely follow his conviction. Oh ! how sad ! Father,
let me go and plead with Gen. Butler for brother.   It
may be, that his heart will relent.   When we saw him,
ill humor may have been in the ascendant; or to enforce
obedience, he may have sought to excite terror.   You
know that men like such displays. Will you let me go,
father ?

Aug. B. Daughter, he is a heartless man. It will
avail nothing.

Belle B. O, father ! soft words of entreaty may melt a
heart of stone.   There are few men so cold, so indiffer-

ent to human suffering, who will not listen to a woman's appeal for mercy. Gen. Butler knows that brother is not a spy. Why then, bring him to trial for that offence? You know that to be tried by a Military Commission is conviction. I would go and appeal to his sense of justice, and if he have any, to his feelings of pity. It can do no harm, at least; let me go.

Eugene B. (Rising on his crutches,) It can do no good; and rather would I risk the consequences of trial than you be again brought in contact with that vile beast.

Belle B. Oh! brother why do you talk thus!
Your life and my happiness are at stake;
Let me make the trial.

(A knock at the door; Maj. Whitley announced by servant and enters; *Exit* Belle Beaumont.)

Maj. W. (Addressing A. Beaumont.) I wish to see you alone. (*Exit* Eugene B.) Your son and Rennier are to be tried by a Military Commission; it may be within a few hours. Mumford's trial is over. Orders have been issued for the removal of your son hence to prison.

Aug. B. O! this cruel war! am I to become its victim in mine old age? My only son to be taken from me! Can not I be spared this affliction? Surely, surely, the General does not desire to have my child murdered? If he be tried, his conviction follows. No one escapes.

Maj. W. The General has been very much wounded by the treatment which he has received from the people of this city, and especially the ladies, and is therefore not much in the humor of mercy. He believes that it is necessary to make examples.

Aug. B. But to deter from crime, the guilty only should be punished—not the innocent.

Maj. W. True, but who is to judge? The Court, I suppose.

Aug. B. But these trials have sunk into mere formalities—to accuse, is to convict.

Maj. W. Too true—one of the fruits of rebellion and civil commotion.

Aug. B. Right, I am afraid.

Maj. W. Gen. Butler will most certainly send these

young men before a Military Commission unless they should escape.

Aug. B. How could they escape?

Maj. W. A very remote contingency, I grant you, but one that is possible.

Aug. B. Possible! by what means?

Maj. W. Were I to tell you, it would probably avail nothing.

Aug. B. Aye, it will—if it be possible.

Maj. W. Give me that pledge, and I will tell you.

Aug. B. Upon honor, you have it.

Maj. W. Your riches are represented to be very great.

Aug. B. It is a mistake, sir.

Maj. W. Lands and houses, stocks, bonds, and other securities, gold and silver plate, gold and silver coin, paintings, a cellar that would make the eyes of Bacchus sparkle with delight—these are all said to be yours.

Aug. B. An exaggerated account—altogether exaggerated. When the war broke out, I was, it is true, in comfortable circumstances, but what a change! I have had to dispose of property to enable me to live,—had taxes to pay—had to invest in Confederate securities—bonds and notes, which are already fearfully depreciated in value, and may in the end be worth nothing. O! no, sir, I am greatly reduced. I will have hardly any thing left.

Maj. W. If that be so, it is unfortunate for these young men.

Aug. B. Rennier is only a friend of my son, and his guest at my house.

Maj. W. Their fortunes are linked together; the fate of one will be the fate of the other. What would save one, would save the other.

Aug. B. How can that be done, is the question.

Maj. W. To speak frankly, you can save them if you will.

Aug. B. I will do it then.

Maj. W. You will have to pay for it.

Aug. A. To whom?

Maj. W. To me.

Aug. B. But the ransom may be too great?

Maj. W. You are able to pay it.

Aug. B. I have already told you that I have been greatly reduced by the war.

Maj. W. Not much ; your money and valuables have been secreted.

Aug. B. (Much agitated.) My money and valuables !

Maj. W. They may be found—I doubt not.

Aug. B. (Aside.) Betrayed by my servants !

Maj. W. To conclude this matter. Your gold and silver coin—your plate—a selection from your paintings, and a goodly proportion of the contents of your cellar will secure the release of these young men.

Aug. B. Would you impoverish a poor old man and his two children—in part, too, for the ransom of a stranger ?

Maj. W. You will have plenty left.

Aug. B. (Aside.) Does he know about the concealment of my treasure ?—if I only knew that ?

You say I have money and valuables secreted. Why have they not been seized ? I understand the Commanding General has made many seizures of the kind.

Maj. W. I prefer to make my gains by bargain and sale, and not in that way. Gen. Butler has nothing to do with my trades.

Aug. B. But you might not be able to have the young men released, should you bargain to do so—certainly not without the General's consent.

Maj. W. They shall be released from confinement, and brought here before the ransom is delivered. What say you ? I must leave.

Aug. B. I must consider of this.

Maj. W. You will have time to consider before my return. We must then close this business. (Proceeds to leave the room.)

Aug B. As I am interested only in the liberty of my son, will you not abate half your demand for his release alone ?

Maj. W. You have heard my terms—they will not be changed. [*Exit.*

Aug. B. (Solus.) Knows that I have money and valuables secreted ! If that be true, then, I had as well surrender them. But he don't know—he only suspects this. That is the secret of the proposed bargain. It is an attempt to black-mail me. But the life of my son is in their hands. I am powerless. O, this traffic in blood! it is monstrous ! monstrous ! what am I to do ? To be reduced to poverty in my old age—to be made penniless —become an object of charity ! This is the price to be paid for the redemption of my son, who is guilty of no crime! I can't pay it; (pauses,) I recall my words; I will think more of it.

SCENE III.

Private house, New Orleans. Mrs. Campbell, lady of the house, seated in her parlor.

(Enter gentleman and lady.)

Mrs. C. My dear Julia, I am so glad to see you! glad always, but oh! in these troublous times, to meet with a sympathetic heart is such a source of happiness; (addressing gentleman) do be seated. My dear sir, how happy am I to meet you and Julia. Now, I have had a presentiment of this visit—all this day I have been expecting some dear friend, and, Julia, you are that person. I am in such distress—turned out of my house and driven to take shelter in this little cuddy. But I won't allow myself to grow crazy about it. Julia, do they let you keep your house?

Julia. No, Annie, we are now looking for a house; have just received notice to vacate ours.

Annie. Companions then in distress, which makes our sympathies mutual. Julia, have you heard how they treated me?

Julia. Only that you had been turned out of your house—no particulars.

Annie. Then, you have heard little. The Commanding General first gave me notice (my husband being absent from the city) that he would want my house for public use. The very next day, while we were about sitting down to dinner, he drove up in a carriage, his wife with him, and guarded by an escort of soldiers, and demanded my keys. Of course, I could do nothing but deliver them to him. They then went through the house from cellar to garret—examined every room; opened my closets and wardrobes, looked into every thing, the most private places; and after satisfying themselves, gave me notice to vacate the house immediately, or prepare to have others quartered with me. O, Julia, I never wanted to be a man as I did then. But I took it all quietly. I couldn't help myself; and next day I got this little house, and brought what I could of my furniture and goods here, but I have left the greater part behind, which I may never see again.

Julia. Why did he seize your house—he had one already?

Annie. Because ours was a finer house ; and he wanted to put one of his officers in Gen. Twiggs', the one he was occupying. And what do you think? He ordered all the servants to remain on the premises, and between threats and promises, prevailed on all but one, to do so.

Julia. The reason given for taking our house is the same—to accommodate an officer and his family, but I fear, Annie, to be put to much worse uses, from what I am informed others have been put to. Oh ! what a horrid thought !

Annie. You and Mr. Martell are so welcome, and as Mayor Munro is to be here with some friends to talk about the sad condition of affairs, do remain ; the hour has nearly arrived. Let us try to take comfort from common counsels, in our common sufferings. I hear them coming now.

(Enter Mayor Munro and citizens.)

Mayor M. My dear madam, I hope I find you well. You know these gentlemen, I believe—Mr. and Mrs. Martell—glad to meet you. (Addressing Mrs. C.) I received your note, and I am most happy to offer you the benefit of my counsel in these days of trouble. I hope that in you changed condition, you are comfortable, at least.

Mrs. C. O, yes ! I shall not complain of the inconveniences to which I have been put, if it should end at this. But what may not be expected of a man who would issue such an order as the one which appeared in this morning's Delta, aimed at helpless woman? In infamy it is without a parallel. The savage wreaks vengeance upon his victim by torture and death ; but this is worse than either. No woman is now safe from insult at home or on the streets. Oh ! I have not language to express my abhorrence of this outrage upon my sex. No paper that contains this order shall come into my house.

Mayor M. What you say is but too true. In company with a number of gentlemen—these present were of the number—I called upon the General commanding to ask a revocation, or at least a modification of that order. It was refused, and we were dismissed in the most insulting manner.   We have however, sent to him a protest against the order, but with little hope that it will accomplish any good result.

Mrs. C. Then, what are we to do?   We are at the mercy of this cruel-hearted tyrant.   I am here with my little children, and one servant—and how long she can be relied on, no one can tell.   The intimacy of the soldiers with the servants has corrupted them to such an extent that they can no longer be trusted.   Their feelings have, in this way, been alienated from us, and they have been made believe that we are their worst enemies.

1st cit. The condition of things, in my part of the city, has become most intolerable.   The servants who remain have not only become disagreeable on account of their insolence, but refuse to do any work, except as it may please them ; and should you dismiss one, you are exposed to arrest and punishment.   Several of my neighbors—old men—have been sent to the chain-gang for this offence—I have seen them working on the streets with ball and chain.

2d cit. The same case in my part of the city.

3d cit. In mine the same, and I believe every where.

1st cit. And this confiscation order is depriving many of the means of living.   The oath of allegiance is no protection.   Pretexts of all sorts are invented to deprive one of its benefits.   Want of loyalty, which can be proved, at any time, by a suborned negro witness, if a low white man is not found for the business ; the pretence of the necessity of feeding the starving poor, and a thousand other schemes, are devised for plundering you.   If you should not meet the requisitions made upon you in coin, which the fewest number now can do, your property is at the mercy of these officials—especially your plate, if you have any, down even to a spoon.   Mr. Mayor, where is this to end, and what are we to do ?

Mayor M. Where it is to end, is beyond the reach of my forecast, except in the worst of consequences.   What we are to do, I can answer more satisfactorily to myself. We have, in my opinion, but one course to pursue, viz : to avoid all public demonstration of our feelings, and bear the ills that are upon us with all the fortitude and patience that we can summon, with the hope that the Government at Washington will become ashamed of the administration of affairs here.   It has already shocked the moral sense of the civilized nations, who are lookers-

on of this contest.   The opinion of the world may work
a change for us.   That is my hope.   With a military
man here, actuated purely by the motive of duty, and
governed by a sense of justice and humanity, we would
have little trouble ; but the officer now in command is a
mere politician, seeking advancement on that line only.
And he is made worse—more cruel, by the fear that
moderation and feelings of humanity shown in his administration of affairs, might lead to a suspicion of his
party fealty.   You know he acted with the Democratic
party before the war.

    2d cit. In your judgment, I fully concur.

    1st cit. So do I.

    3d cit. Then we are all agreed.

    Mrs. C. What else to do, I can not myself see ;
But this insult, the peril of outrage
To which, by this order, we are exposed,
Cries aloud to Heaven for swiftest vengeance;
It had been better, if, on the sad day,
When o'er our heads was flaunted that curs'd flag,
With torches we had sprung into the streets,
And with our burning homes the sky illumin'd ;
To be driven from home counts but little ;
To be robb'd of plate, or precious jewels,
Is not to be compared with this base thing,
Against which Nature herself pleads revolt.
Woman that I am, to ease accustom'd,
And no want to know, rather would I meet
War's rude shock, and face battle's fiery storm,
And move amidst red slaughter's ghastly scenes,
Than bear this cruel humiliation.

    Mayor M. You speak nobly, madam ; but to what we
cannot prevent or avoid, we must submit.   Resistance to
the authority set over us, or even calling it in question,
would only greater evils upon us entail.

    1st cit. You are right—let us remain quiet, and wait
for better times.

    2d cit. I concur.

    3d cit. So do I.

    Mrs. C. I will be advised by you, and so will we all,
but to submit to this necessity goes like cold steel to my
heart.

•

ACT IV.

SCENE I.

Headquarters.   Gen. Butler and Col. Strong.

Col. S. I have a communication from Mayor Munro,
which I have been requested to hand you. (Hands to
Gen. B. the paper.)

Gen. B. (Reading paper.) A protest from Mayor Munro and other citizens against General Order No. 28;
most insulting and impertinent! Send a summons to
Mayor Munro to attend at these Headquarters forthwith.
[*Exit* Col. Stroug.

(Enter A. J. Butler.)

A. J. B. How fares it with you, brother?

Gen. B. Well; but am devilishly annoyed. General
Order No. 28 seems to have raised h—ll throughout the
city. It has set every petticoat, it seems, to shaking, as
if the wearers had the ague. If it wasn't for these devil-
ish women, I could quiet the rebels of the other gender.
Munro and a party of citizens have just been here to ask
for a qualification of the order. I dismissed them with
contempt ; and now here comes a protest from the same
parties, couched in most insulting terms. I have sent
for him, and when he appears, he shall answer for this
insulting paper. Well, how are things going on above?
I hear that there is quite a stir about my orders regulat-
ing the plantations.

A. J. B. There was at first a little stir, but things have
quieted down. The negroes were generally leaving, and
the plantations would have been stripped of labor, but
for your orders. The presence of the soldiers now keeps
them in order ; and they are working very well. I have
made contracts about the division of crops with a good
many sugar and cotton planters—which could never
have been made but for these orders. By judicious arrangements for the distribution of supplies, under your
orders to prevent starvation, I have secured a considera-
ble quantity of cotton.

Gen. B. How many bales, think you?

A. J. B. About ten thousand.

Gen. B. That will do very well. The permits for provisions which covered the saltpetre, powder, muskets, and other war material sent to the rebels, worked like a charm, eh ?

A. J. B. Just so.

Gen. B. Have you got off the furniture, pianos, paintings, &c., and the confiscated goods which you bought ? I am afraid we shall be short of transportation.

A. J. B. Transportation is amply sufficient. I have taken the precaution to consign the pianos and silver plate, &c., in foreign bottoms, to Havana.

Gen. B. A good idea. That was sharp.

(Enter Col. Strong.)

Col. S. Mayor Munro, in reply to your summons here, says : " Tell Gen. Butler my office is at the City Hotel, where he can see me, if desirable."

Gen. B. Then order his arrest and confinement in Fort Jackson. Include the whole party who were here with him. I will put them where they may plot treason at their leisure. Issue the order forthwith.

[*Exit* Col. Strong.

Gen. B. Has Whitley said any thing to you about the spies within our lines—one of them the son of a rich old Creole in the city ?

A. J. B. He has ; and I think he has an appointment at the old gentleman's house to-night—at least very soon. We understand the case perfectly, and will work it up. Whitley is a trump.

Gen. B. The very fellow for us. Now, Andrew, we don't know how long we shall be here. We must make hay while the sun shines. This is a fine field for us. We may make our jack if you play the game right—you and Whitley. As for the Provost Marshal and such nincompoops, they are not worth considering. We will use them.

A. J. B. You are right. Business presses, and I must go, but before I go, here is a requisition for supplies which I desire you to approve. (Handing papers to Gen. B., which he signs.)   [*Exit* A. J B.

Headquarters. New Orleans.

(Enter Gen. Butler and Col. Strong.)

Col. S. I have to report the re-arrest of Mrs. Phillips, this time for insulting the remains of Lieut. DeKay, when his funeral procession was passing her house.

Gen. B. Order her into my presence immediately. She is a mischievous woman. I will put her where she will not repeat such insults. By-the-way, Colonel, the British Consul interposed in behalf of the Florences, and I thought it best to return the plate seized on board the ship. It was claimed by a son-in-law, Dr. Crawcour, who turns out to be a British subject. We have enough on our hands without putting the old Lion to growling. But the swords which were presented to Miss Florence by Gen. Twiggs, on leaving the city, will be retained. One of them was presented to him by Congress, and will be highly prized. She is certainly a most incorrigible rebel. I had to threaten her with arrest before she would give up the swords.

I came near forgetting it—you will issue an order concerning the clergy of this city. I have been informed that a day of fasting and thanksgiving is to be observed in obedience to some supposed proclamation of one Jefferson Davis, in the several churches of this city. I learn also, that prayers are offered up by some of these rebel clergy, for the success of rebel arms, and the destruction of the Union, and that the Episcopal clergy have left out the prayer prescribed in their liturgy for the President of the United States and Congress, and put in a prayer for Jeff Davis and his rebel Congress. Now, I will put a stop to all this. I am no Puritan, and don't care a d—n for the prayers of these fellows, *per se.* But there is to be no fasting and praying in obedience to Jeff's proclamations. These Episcopalians shall pray for old Abe, though it may do him no good, which is highly probable Issue orders covering all these points, and I will execute them to the letter. Let Mrs. Philips be brought in.   [*Exit* Col. Strong.

(Enter Mrs. Phillips, under guard.)

Gen. B. (Addressing Mrs. P.) I regret that it has been

found necessary to put you under arrest again. But your offence could not be overlooked. Is it true that you laughed and mocked at the remains of Lieutenant DeKay, as the funeral procession passed your house ?

Mrs. P. It could hardly be thought that a lady would make a public exhibition of herself in the manner you state. But at the hour when the procession passed, I was in company with some ladies on my balcony, and "was in good spirits that day."

Gen. B. Have you no excuse to offer for this insult ?

Mrs. P. I have not, if an insult was given.

Gen. B. I have had you brought before me to answer this charge.

Mrs. P. I have answered it.

Gen. B. Aye, and by repeating the insult !

Mrs. P. You say so.

Gen. B. I do say so, and I will punish you.

Mrs. P. I don't doubt it.

Gen. B. Then you will not be disappointed?

Mrs. P. I shall not.

Gen. B. But I will not pass upon your case without hearing your defence. Had you read General Order No. 28 before this occurrence ?

Mrs. P.

Yes ! and the blood rush'd wildly to my heart;
I wonder'd that the brain that conceiv'd it
Had not, in God's wrath, stopp'd its workings,
And the hand that wrote it had not wither'd
While inditing the foul record of shame.

Gen. B. Let this talk cease. Have you any thing to say why you should not be punished for this insult?

Mrs. P. Any thing to say ? worst of hateful tyrants !
Thou, who hast won immortal infamy,
Dishonor'd his country's fame and her flag !
Thou, who hast made war on helpless woman !
Insulted her, to licens'd lust expos'd
And outrage by a brutal soldiery !
Thou who hast won the loathsome name of beast !
I defy thy pow'r—send me to prison—
Do thy will ; I'll glory in the honor
Of being first victim to this Order.

Gen. B. Take the crazy woman away. But hold—here is the order, which I have already prepared in her case, and which you will hand to Col. Strong. I will send her to a good place for lunatics, and under good

keepers—to Ship Island, there to be confined till further
orders.   [*Exit* guard, with Mrs. Philips.

SCENE III.

Headquarters.   Gen. Butler, solus.

(Enter Belle Beaumont, followed by a sentinel.)

Gen. B. (Rising.) I think I recognize Miss Beau-
mont, who accompanied her father here ?
Belle B. Yes, unknown to him, hither have I come,
Unattended, to beg for my brother ;
And to thy sense of pity to appeal.
He is young, and if amiss has acted,
'Twas from youth's ardor and indiscretion,
In answ'ring the call of his State to arms;
It was the error of noble impulse,
Patriotic, misguided tho' it may've been.
Look at the intent, the essence of crime,
And in mercy his conduct do forgive !
O ! General, thou hast a father's heart ;
Let a father's love move thee to pity
For the sorrows of a stricken household !
Last night, in my dreams, a sainted mother
Visited me, and with tears besought me
This last appeal for mercy to offer.
For this I come, and would kneel before thee (kneeling)
To reach its promise—my brother's freedom.
O ! hear a sister's appeal for mercy !
O ! be mov'd by woman's tears !
Gen. B. Arise, young lady ; this posture suits thee
Ne'er so well as standing ; then thy beauty
Doth appear in its fullest measure.
Belle B. In this heart compliments have no response;
They serve now only to deepen its sorrow.
Gen. B.
Such charms, as thou hast in form and feature,
Will ne'er fail the will of their possessor
Any enterprize of love or ambition
To attempt, and crown with glorious success.
Belle B. (Aside.) O ! this is too cruel !
Pray, sir, do not treat my petition thus ;
Thy words of flatt'ry make me more wretched.
Gen. B. Dear young lady, my meaning thou mistak'st,
To speak of thy charms is far from flatt'ry ;

2

Cold as this heart is call'd, their radiance
Its springs hath thaw'd, and a new-born passion
My blood doth stir, and would have utterance.
                                    [*Exit* Miss B.
But; the vision of beauty is dissolved;
Like the frightened fawn she fled my approach;
Perhaps 'tis best; my judgment was at fault;
Are these New Orleans women all like her?
Then, the South's hot blood is temper'd so high
That naught that's base hath admixture with it;
But, why do I speculate on this theme?
I have graver matters than love on hand.
            [Seats himself and takes up manuscript.
The Military Commission has convicted Mumford.
What else could it do? To be hanged is a terrible sen-
tence I have a thought to offer him a commutation of
punishment, upon condition that he will take the oath of
allegiance, which his conduct before me, and at his trial,
shews he will not do. But the offer will have a show of
humanity. I can first sound him without making the
offer directly.
            [Summons Col. Strong, who enters.
I will not yet approve Mumford's sentence. Have
him brought before me again.
    Col. S. (Handing Gen. B. a paper.) Here is a petition
in his behalf from ladies.   [*Exit* Col. Strong.
    Gen. B. (Solus.) It looks as if I shall never get rid of
these infernal women. They are sticking their fingers
into every thing. I will no longer be bothered with
them and their petitions. (Throws petition under the
table.) My mind is already made up.

        (Enter guard with Mumford.)

    Gen. B. Have you knowledge of your conviction?
    M. The trial itself assured that.
    Gen. B. You have had a fair trial before honorable
and just men.
    M. As fair as foregone judgment would allow.
    Gen. B. I have not approved the sentence yet.
    M. Not with your sign-manual, you mean.
    Gen. B. I have not affixed that evidence of approval,
because pardon might follow penitence. Abjuration of
the cause you lately espoused, and allegiance to your
Government—would you offer this to secure mitigation
of sentence?

M. My country's cause abjure, her flag disown !
To her invading foe, swear allegiance !
Dumb as the mute rock, may Heaven strike me,
E'er these lips pronounce the traitorous words.
I have much to live for, but at this price,
Life would be a burden, its hopes all dead ;
Its smiling fields become a blasted heath,
And I a wanderer o'er the desert scene.
I've a wife and child to love and cherish ;
I've friends, and am not without ambition ;
All these—life itself, I will here resign,
Rather than for them my honor barter,
And the cause of my native land betray.
My last prayer shall be that yonder flag,
That now floats over this once proud city,
May find another hand to haul it down ;
And that the stars and bars be rais'd again,
To wave in triumph o'er a fre'd people.

Gen. B. You then reject my offer—the mercy tendered you. Well, you have no one to blame but yourself for the consequences. Let the prisoner be remanded. Orderly, send the Adjutant General to me.

(Enter Col. Strong.)

Gen. B. (Taking up paper, writing.) I have no alternative but to approve the finding of the Military Commission in Mumford's case. He will have to hang, and I think the sooner, the better—for example's sake. Order the necessary preparations, and let him be executed within the next twenty-four hours. (*Exit* Col. Strong.) (Solus.) He seems to court his doom. He aspires to the patriotism of the old Romans, which in these days nobody but a fool would.

ACT V.

SCENE I.

Beaumont's house. Aug. Beaumont and Maj. Whitley.

Maj. W. I come to conclude the matter of your son and his young friend. What say you ?

Aug. B. You said that I had money and valuables se-creted. Whence did you get this information ?

Maj. W. My dear sir ! nothing can be gained by this inquiry. The fate of these young men is in your hands. Terms have been offered ; will you accept them ? I have come here to act, not to talk. To win your favor to this view I have no argument. It is for you to decide.

Aug. B. The ransom is too heavy, beyond my means. I am too poor.

Maj. W. That is for you to decide; (rises to leave) my time is precious.

Aug. B. The ransom of Rennier you still require? He is only the friend of my son.

Maj. W. My terms have been made known to you ; I must leave

(Enter Belle Beaumont.)

Belle B. I trust that I am not intruding—did you send for me, father ?

Aug. B. I did not, but am glad you have come. This is my daughter, Maj. Whitley. Do you object to her knowing the object of this interview and its present state ?

Maj. W. I do not.

Aug. B. (Addressing his daughter Belle,) Maj. Whit-ley, who is high in authority, proffers to save Eugene and young Rennier, upon certain terms, viz : that I should pay a large ransom ; all the coin and plate, I am possessed of, a selection from my paintings, and a divis-ion of the cellar. I tell him that young Rennier is only the friend of Eugene, made my guest by the accident of war, and that obligation does not require me to ransom him. Besides Belle, I am not able to comply with the terms. It would reduce me and my children to poverty.

I am now too old for such dire calamity, and it would be so cruel to you. Eugene might work his way in the world, but how could you?

Belle B. What is your answer to Maj. Whitley?

Aug. B. I have given no positive answer, and he is about leaving.

Belle B. I would say something to father about this, but with your pleasure I would have only his ear.

Aug. B. (Addressing Maj. Whitley,) Will you walk into another parlor and await our interview?

Maj. W. Certainly, sir.

Exeunt Aug. B. and Maj. Whitley.

Belle B. (Solus.) If my voice is heeded, the bargain shall be made. Father is loth to pay the ransom, I know. His riches he has himself earn'd, and that makes them more his own; and to be robbed by duress of this sort is hard, indeed. But if by submitting to this demand, poverty should be my fate, I would do it.

(Enter Aug. Beaumont.)

Aug. B. Belle, what do you think of this offer of ransom? Strange he will not make separate terms for Eugene. He insists upon a ransom for Rennier also. Besides, I think it is a most outrageous attempt at extortion. He wants to black-mail me. He don't, in words, say that he knows where my treasure is secreted, but by insinuation he would make me believe that he does. I have doubts about this. He has, in my opinion, had Eugene and Rennier arrested merely to extort money from me; and I have almost made up my mind to take the risks. After all, there may be no trial. The General and Maj. Whitley may be in partnership in this transaction. I have strong suspicions that this is the truth.

Belle B. If that be so, it makes it so much the worse. With such an understanding between them, there would be little hope of accommodation without complying with their demands.

Aug. B. But if Eugene is not to be tried, then this ransom will be so much paid for nothing—mere extortion—downright robbery, worse than the highwayman, who says, " stand and deliver." There is at least boldness in that. The demand amounts, in value, to near one hundred thousand dollars. He excepts part of the paintings and cellar, the least valuable to me.

Belle B. Father, if you believed that Eugene would

be tried, unless you acceded to this arrangement, would you do it?

Aug. B. Well, yes; but, then, it would make me a pauper. Belle, you asked my permission to make another appeal to Gen. Butler. It may be that you can at last touch his feelings of pity, and cause him to relent. To save this great sacrifice of property, and consequent poverty, all effort should be exhausted.

Belle B. I know that such an appeal would avail nothing.

Aug. B. Then, I fear that there is no hope; but how do you know this, my child?

Belle B. I know it.

Aug. B. But how do you know it?

Belle B. I know it well; I have attempted what
You opposed, but that you do now advise.
Without your knowledge, alone I have gone,
And on bended knee, for mercy pleaded,
But with insult, my pray'r was rejected.
The presence of the base tyrant I fled,
As I would the death-breathing pestilence.
O, father! "he knows no touch of pity,"
Who now lords it o'er this fallen city;
Sympathy for its people, he feels none;
To compass his ends, crimes most appalling,
Murder, even, would be lightly esteem'd.
All hope of mercy from your mind dispel;
To move his heart, an angel's tongue would fail.

Aug. B. I fear 'tis too true. It may be best for me to accept the proffered terms; but why should I pay ransom for Rennier?

Belle B. No natural tie binds you to do this, but he is brother's friend, and your guest, and that is enough to have his ransom insisted on.

Aug. B. Well, I will go for Maj. Whitley, and close the bargain. But, Belle, it will be our ruin. I will then be a poor man, and you the daughter of one. Poverty stares us in the face, and the world's charity will mock at our calamity.   [*Exit* Aug. Beaumont.

(Enter Aug. B. and Maj. Whitley.)

Aug. B. Well, as hard as the bargain is, I have decided to accept it. When can they be set free?

Maj. W. I will have Rennier here in less than a half hour, and they may pass the lines to-night, if they will.

Aug. B. Be in haste, then.   [*Exit* Whitley.

Aug. B. Belle, I am afraid that this is a sad business for us.   It will matter little with me, whose life is now a mere point, incapable of measurement; but you, my daughter, have long years before you.

Belle B. Father, say no more.   Bewail not my future; I am content.   This is the happiest moment of my life. Eugene at liberty, and Clarence Rennier to be—his companion; to enjoy the fruits of this ransom.   This accomplished, welcome poverty, with all its ills!

Aug. B. We must have the means at hand to conclude the bargain with this extortioner when he returns. But I can shew him the place of deposit; the premises already being guarded, he can remove things at his pleasure.   He will no doubt agree to this.

SCENE II.

A. Beaumont's house.

Auguste Beaumont, Belle Beaumont, Eugene Beaumont, Clarence Rennier, and Maj. Whitley.

Maj. W. To prevent suspicion, and secure a safe retreat, it would be well that they leave the city before dawn of day.   But the arrangement is not complete. The consideration coming to me is not delivered, nor placed within my power.   This is a condition precedent.

Aug. B. Come with me.

[*Exeunt* Aug. Beaumont and Maj. Whitley.

Eugene B. As this agreement is already made, I make no objection, tho' I could not have advised it.   'Tis true, father has property left sufficient to keep him above want, but he will never take that view of it; the misery of threatened poverty will, with him, equal the reality.

Belle B. But, brother, the fate that awaited you would have made him more unhappy.

Eugene B. Well, I must begin to pack up.

[*Exit* Eugene B.

Clarence Rennier.

I have seen thy hand in my deliv'rance;
For this, how can I ever repay thee?
The pledge of my love, thou hast already;
What more in return, can this heart offer?
Speak quick; time is now on its swiftest wing.
Hast thou words to comfort me e'er we part?

Without these, my liberty hath no joy.
Rather would I to prison walls return,
Than go hence without promise of thy love;
That would cheer my heart in this night's journey,
And in all the dark days that may follow;
And whene'er the fortunes of war permit,
Bring me again to thy side; the moments fly—
Have I thy promise?

Belle B. Thy liberty involved my happiness; this achieved, that may follow, should not the fortunes of war separate us forever.

Rennier. May Heaven avert the alternative!
My happiness is now complete, but disturb'd,
(Strange paradox!) and by one thought only—
To leave thee under the cruel tyrant,
Whose iron hand this city oppresses.
Our parting is thus made doubly painful;
But the dark clouds, which now o'erhang our sky,
May soon pass away, and sweet sunshine cheer
The hearts of our people with brighter hopes;
Then, may we meet and rob from cruel war,
The seal of happiness it now denies.
Farewell!   [*Exit* Rennier.

Belle B. (Solus.)
I may ne'er see him more; his proud spirit
Would his countr'ys wrongs and his own avenge;
To battle's perils he will be expos'd;
And on some bloody field, the fatal ball
May speed to his heart, and his life's-blood draw;
Or within gloomy prison walls confin'd,
Far from friends, he may pine away and die.
Oh! this cruel war, would that it were o'er!
With its sighs and sorrows—its world of woes!

(Enter Aug. Beaumont and Maj. Whitley.)

Maj. W. All is now arranged; this paper will pass the young men through the lines. It has the Commanding General's signature. You have my thanks for your courtesy and kindness.   [*Exit* Maj. Whitley.

Aug. B. Thanks for courtesy and kindness! Rob a poor old man, and thank him for the opportunity! Well, my child, the affair is now ended, and it may be for the best; I hope so. The boys must now get off.

SCENE III.

Headquarters.

Gen. Butler, Col. Strong, Capt. Davis, and Capt. Brennan.

Gen. B. Orderly! (enters orderly) Some brandy and
water. (Which he serves—all drink.)

I have had a hint from Washington that the difficulty
with Count Mejan and with these other d—d little con-
suls has been made the pretext of my enemies to assail
me. But the Government ought to know that these officials have been aiding and abetting the rebels ever since
the occupation of the city. It has been my object to put
a stop to this; but if I am interfered with, the fault lies
with my superiors. My explanation of the affair to
Commissioner Johnston while here, seemed to satisfy
him. I shewed him that Count Mejan, indeed nearly
every foreign Consul here, had violated the laws of neutrality. But his case is the most serious of all. He has
covered by his flag all manner of illegal and hostile
transactions; connived at the delivery of clothing for the
Rebel Army, and removed from the city nearly half a
million of specie to supply its wants in the field. These
were certainly gross violations of neutrality; but President Lincoln, in his anxiety to avoid complications with
foreign powers, may be inclined to yield the point which
I made. If so, I have nothing further to say. He is
my superior, and the responsibility rests with him. If
he permits these representatives of foreign governments
to become the allies of the rebels—be it so.

Col. S. I hardly think that the President will interfere
with you. Thus far, all your acts have been approved
at Washington—that is my information.

Gen. B. Yes; I have been well supported by the War
Department. The rumor, to which I refer, may be un-
founded—probably is.

Have you (addressing Col. Strong) issued the order
preventing druggists from furnishing medicines to the
Confederate soldiers in the city?

Col. S. I have.

Gen. B. That is right. Such persons must go to our
Medical Director, and take the oath of allegiance before
being served. Have you all preparations made for the

execution of Mumford, and a sufficient force detailed to prevent a rescue ? I have heard that "the thugs, roughs, rowdies and gamblers have held a meeting and solemnly resolved that he shall not be executed."

Col. S. All necessary preparations for the occasion have been made.

(Wife of Mumford and his little daughter announced by card, handed by Orderly.)

Gen. B. Well, I'll be d—d if the women don't worry me out of my life. Now here comes Mumford's wife and daughter. I can do nothing for them. Bid them come in. (To Orderly.) [*Exit* Orderly.

(Enter Mrs. Mumford and daughter.)

[*Exit* Col. Strong and Staff officers.

Mrs. Mumford.
For the thoughts that rush to my swimming brain,
In this sad hour, my tongue hath no utt'rance.
In my distress, my own voice I scarce know ;
My poor husband is condemned to die ;
But the manner of his death, to be hanged,
As a felon—this pierces his proud heart.
To fall beneath the death-dealing volley,
Were naught compar'd to this ignominy.
Thou art a soldier, and a soldier's pride
Feelest; wilt thou this last request refuse ?
No ; if a soldier's pulse throbs in thy veins,
It beats in unison with this appeal ;
What I ask, surely thou *wilt* not deny,
That he die like a soldier—be not hang'd.
His poor orphan child and widow'd mother,
From this altern'tive, would some comfort take ;
Wilt thou grant it ? it is all that he asks.

Gen. B. It is his request, is it ?

Mrs. M. It is.

Gen. B. Then, for that reason, it will be denied. Had it been yours only, it might have been considered. But even in that aspect, I can't see the difference to a widow, whether her husband had been hanged or shot. In either event, the opportunity of getting another would be the same.

Mrs. M. To honor my husband—my children love,
To household duties all my time to give,
Has been my fondest pride and my glory ;

More than this to do I have ne'er aspired.
Favor from those in place and pow'r to seek
By flattery's arts I am not suited ;
But an insult to resent, I have strength,
And the daring to speak the scorn I feel
For him a helpless woman thus would wound.
Base as thou hast been, nothing hast thou done,
With this most wanton insult can compare;

(Enter Orderly with dispatch, which Gen. B. receives
and reads.)

The Savage, with reason's faintest ray endow'd,
The lowest, meanest of created souls,
To such degradation hath ne'er fallen ;
With vengeance by thine enemies pursued ;
By those, whose favor thou art now courting
For selfish ends, betrayed and despised,
May Heaven's with'ring curse be henceforth thine,
And thy name, in letters of scorn, be graved,
On history's page, forever to be link'd
With all that's base and mean in human-kind.

[*Exit* Mrs. M.

Gen. B. My worst fears are realized. and at this hour !
My Government strikes me down, while the curse of that
woman is ringing in mine ears.   What ! removed from
my command ?   No—to be relieved by Banks !   The
same thing.   (Reading dispatch :)

" The Commanding General has evidently acted under a misapprehension, to be referred to the patriotic
zeal which governs him, to the circumstances encircling
his command, at the time so well calculated to excite
suspicion, and to an earnest desire to punish to the extent of his supposed power, all who had contributed, or
were contributing, to the aid of a rebellion the most un-
justifiable and wicked that insane or bad men ever engaged in."

Misapprehension to be referred to patriotic zeal !   In
other words, that I am a zealous patriot, but a fool !
That is the English of it.   Why, I would rather be
charged with want of patriotism than be called a fool !
With all my faults, I have never been called, fool !
Fool ! why I would rather be called knave, thief, liar,
cut-throat, any thing—even beast !   And this is my re-
ward for service to the country !   What more striking

proof of the ingratitude of Republics? I, who found
this city captured, but not surrendered ; conquered, but
not orderly : I, who restored order, punished crime ;
opened commerce ; fed a starving people ; reformed the
currency, and gave protection to all. I, who could have
turned over the property of this city to indiscriminate
"loot," like the palace of the Emperor of China ; I, who
could have ordered its sons to have been blown from
cannon like the Sepoys of Delhi ; I, who have levied upon the wealthy rebels, and paid out nearly half a million
of dollars to feed 40,000 of the starving poor of all nations ; I, who saw that this rebellion was a war of the
aristocrats against the middling men, of the rich against
the poor, of the land-owners — the slave oligarchy
against the laborers, and therefore took the substance of
the wealthy to feed the innocent poor ; I, who have
cleansed out the streets of this city, its canals and public
squares, and demonstrated that the pestilence, by such
means, can be kept from its borders ; I, who, by a simple
order, brought the women of this city to their senses,
and made them treat my officers as gentlemen. I, who
have brought to the gallows the traitor Mumford, who
tore down our national flag, and trailed it in the dust ; I,
who have done all this, and much more, could my mod-
esty allow me to make a parade of my public services,
am now to be superseded—eased off from this command
with honeyed words—compliments to my " patriotic
zeal," rather than to good sense—"patriotic zeal" having
its vent under "misapprehension!" Was there ever such
an act of ingratitude? and such a silly reason given for
it ! Misapprehension ! Who the devil is a better judge
of the condition of things here than I ? I have always
had some credit for brains, an article which I apprehend
does not exceed the demand at Washington. Banks !
Who is he ? A little third-rate lawyer—now a General.
The country is gone to h—ll, if this is to be the policy ;
the Union, the negroes, the armies—every thing ! I enter my solemn protest against this proceeding—this attempt to degrade me. But I am a soldier, and must
obey orders—that is military rule. I have one source of
consolation ; it is the fact, that I have turned the current
of events here to my own material advantage, and that
pricking the bubble, military reputation, does not involve
the loss of that which I have laid up for future comfort.
And it may be, too, that all in the end may turn out

right.   I will go to Washington, and present my case in such a light that in spite of the intrigues of enemies, I shall still be able to ride upon the tide that leads on to fortune.

www.ingramcontent.com/pod-product-compliance
Lightning Source LLC
Chambersburg PA
CBHW030909260626
47169CB00008B/2759